My name is Mark. I am ten years old and I live in Somerset, New Jersey. My family moved here a few months ago from Ohio.

We live in an apartment now, but we are building a new house. The last time we visited the building site my family gave our new home a blessing.

Standing together in a circle, my parents, my sister Nija (NI-jah) and my brother Hakeem (hah-KEEM) and I joined hands and shouted, "Harambe (hah-rahm-BEY)!" This is a Swahili (swah-HEE-lee) word that means, "Let's all pull together."

As a family, we pull together to do many jobs around the house. My chores are to bring in the groceries, pick up the mail, and vacuum.

But I also have time to do things I enjoy—like playing chess with my father.

On December 26 my family begins the celebration of Kwanzaa (KWAHN-zah), a seven-day holiday for African Americans. We set up a special table in our house.

Kwanzaa is an African word that means "first fruits." For a very long time our African ancestors have celebrated the harvest, or gathering, of the first crops. Kwanzaa is a time when we focus on our African-American heritage.

We put seven symbols on the Kwanzaa table. Each symbol stands for something important.

Kinara (kee-NAH-rah) is a candle holder with places for seven candles. It stands for the original African ancestors of African Americans.

Mishumaa Saba (mee-shu-MAH SAH-bah) are seven candles that represent the seven principles of Kwanzaa.

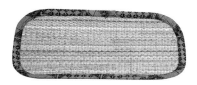

Mkeka (em-KAY-kah) is the mat on which all of the other symbols rest. The mat stands for our history and traditions.

Kikombe Cha Umoja (kee-KOM-bay CHA oo-MOH-jah) is the unity cup. We use it to pour libations for our ancestors, and drink from it as a symbol of unity.

Muhindi (moo-HIN-dee) are ears of dried corn. They stand for the number of children in the family.

Mazao (mah-ZAH-oh) are fruits and vegetables. These represent the outcome of the harvest. The mazao symbolize the good results that come from working together.

Zawadi (zah-WAH-dee) are Kwanzaa gifts. They symbolize the rewards for doing good deeds.

There are many things to do to get ready for Kwanzaa. We make some of the symbols that we place on the table, as well as the zawadi (zah-WAH-dee), the Kwanzaa gifts. My mother and my sister Nija also sew new clothes for each of us.

My father nails some wooden boards together to make into drums. We paint designs in bright colors on the sides.

My mother and Nija sew new clothes from bright African fabrics that my mother has been collecting all year long.

Here, I am helping my father make the candle holder, the kinara. He is showing me how to rub the stain on the wood.

This year Nija is making a book celebrating the seven principles of Kwanzaa to add to the table. These seven principles are: unity, self-determination, collective work and responsibility, cooperative economics, purpose, creativity, and faith.

The seven principles are known as the Nguzo Saba (en-GOO-zoh SAH-bah). They are celebrated during Kwanzaa, but they are guides for living all year long.

One day during Kwanzaa my parents took us to the American Museum of Natural History in New York City. At the museum there was a special Kwanzaa event that celebrated our African heritage. One group that performed was called the Sister Griots. Griot (GREE-oh) means "storyteller." Dancers and musicians helped the griots tell their stories.

On another day my parents took us to a different celebration in New Jersey, where we met a friend of theirs named Dr. Maulana Karenga (Mah-oo-LAH-nah Kah-RAIN-gah). He is the person that created Kwanzaa over 30 years ago.

Dr. Karenga created Kwanzaa so that we can learn about and celebrate our African heritage.

Later, we spent some time in the Kwanzaa market looking at things made in Africa.

On the last day of Kwanzaa our relatives come to our home for a celebration. My grandmother gathers all of us around her and reads us a book about Kwanzaa.

When it is time for our Kwanzaa ceremony to start, I play a drum call. Just as they do in African countries, the drums tell the people that something important is about to happen.

I stand in front of the family with my father as he explains the importance of each symbol on the table. Then, as he lights the candles one by one, I recite the Kwanzaa principles by heart.

After the candles have been lit, Hakeem, Nija, and I provide some entertainment for our family.

Now it is time for the karamu (KAH-rah-moo), the Kwanzaa feast. The table is filled with tasty food.

We serve foods like chicken, candied sweet potatoes, a casserole of broccoli and cauliflower, biscuits, and corn on the cob at our Kwanzaa feast.

After dinner, we exchange the zawadi. The Kwanzaa celebration is over for this year, but its principles stay in our hearts all year long.

We are a strong African-American family.
We are proud of our heritage, proud of
our culture, and proud of ourselves.